To chaser or chase her: A choice between love and alcoholism

By: J.J. Krupitzer

Author introduction:

Hello. This is a book where a man has to choose between the love of his life and booze. Which one will he choose? Well, I guess you're just gonna have to wait for that. As always this is your friend JJ and I am very happy to be writing this book for you. This will be a short Six chapter book. I really hope you enjoy it!

Roger Burns, A 24-year-old, former high school football star and a person who was well liked in the community of Buffalo New York. Now, Roger is a down on his luck alcoholic. Where did it all go wrong? Well, for that we would have to go back to his childhood to see where it all went awry. Would you care to come with me on this journey? If you answered yes, well then you're in for a treat. Roger Burns was born October 5, 1981, in Pittsburgh Pennsylvania to Robert and Anita Burns who moved to Pittsburgh the year before from Omaha Nebraska. Roger was actually born premature, he wasn't supposed to come into the world until December 5, 1981, for some reason he had bigger plans to come into the world a little bit early. Doctors wondered if he would even survive. Surprisingly, Roger turned out to be just fine after a few months of fabulous care from the nurses at McGee women's hospital in Pittsburgh. Anita and Robert were over the moon to be able to take Roger home with them on the day he was actually supposed to be born, December 5, 1981. However, things growing up for Roger weren't getting any easier as because he was born premature, he had a lot of health issues.

Anita and Robert grew increasingly worried as Roger got older, as his health conditions did not improve. Between the seizing and the self abuse, also came the constant night terrors for some reason. There was no reason for the night terrors that they could think of, with that being said they took him to a local pediatrician to see what the problem was. Dr. Tang Chong, A veteran pediatrician of 20 years at Children's Hospital diagnosed him with a moderate form of PTSD. Anita and Robert wondered what could've caused something so traumatic for the little boy as he was just three years old, it was found out later that Roger was sexually assaulted by a close and trusted family friend, 27-year-old Bonnie Plunkett, Plunkett had been a friend of Anita and Robert since high school. They were shocked to learn that someone so close to them could do that to such a small child, when asked about it, Bonnie had no response except to say she was horny and her boyfriend wasn't giving her any so she figured she would take it anyway she could get it. Needless to say, Anita and Robert are more than angry to hear this news and press charges on Plunkett immediately. Bonnie tries to plead insanity at the time she did it, but The judge doesn't buy it and Bonnie Marie Plunkett is sentenced to 50 years in prison for child rape.

After the trial, Anita and Robert never trusted another soul to watch their son again. They knew that he would be too traumatized to let anyone so close to him again. In 1985 at the age of four, Anita and Robert enrolled Roger in Miss Cunningham's School for traumatized children in Pittsburgh's Squirrelhill neighborhood. They figure it will help him tremendously with what he's gone through and he could make friends with kids who have been through the same. The school was run by Miss Abigail Cunningham, a 20-year-old, Blonde haired, enthusiastic young woman who was a victim of child trauma herself. When she was just four years old, she was raped by a trusted family friend by the name of Gregory Stevens, Unfortunately in her case though, Mr. Stevens was never brought to justice and she still is haunted by the memories every day. After graduating early from high school and graduating from slippery rock University with a degree in childhood development, Abigail decided to open up her own school so that she could help kids just like her get through these troubling times. Roger would stay there from 1985 until 1988 when the school had to close down due to the murder of Miss Cunningham. She was found gagged and raped with the words " dirty pig whore" written on her chest in blood on her bathroom floor with the water running, police assumed that she was taking a shower When the assailant attacked her. This is another thing that messed Roger up very badly. He took a real shine to Miss Cunningham and his wife would never be the same after that because he felt that the only woman he had ever trusted is gone now. They tested the semen found on her body and it belongs to an ex-boyfriend of hers by the name of Bob Cratchit, and no not the Bob Cratchit you're thinking of. Cratchet suspected her of cheating with another man so one night he snuck into her house, into her shower had his way with her one last time and killed her. It was evident that Cratchit was A pretty sadistic son of a bitch, he made sure to keep her eyes open and keep the look of terror on her face when the cops arrived. Cratchet felt guilty about nothing and was ordered to stay in trial. At his trial, he was found guilty of not only Abigail's murder but the murder of three other women who were all 20 years old. A memorial service was held for the four girls, Abigail Cunningham, Roberta Fredericks, Bianka Smith and Penny Lane (Little tidbit if there's any Beatles fans out there) all four of the girls were found the same way, Gagged, Raped and something written on their chests in blood. Robert Alexander Cratchit was sentenced to life in prison without the possibility of parole and ordered to serve that sentence in a maximum-security prison.

Anita and Robert contemplated moving out of the Pittsburgh area numerous times throughout the next couple years, the problem was the Burns' Family is not a well-off family, Anita and Robert have to work three and four jobs just to get by. Coupled with medical appointments for Roger, and finding somebody that they trust enough to take care of Roger while they're at work. It became very strenuous for Anita and Robert. However, They knew at some point they had to get Roger out of that city and into what they felt was the safer environment for Roger. Pittsburgh so far had brought them nothing but pain, heartache and suffering, they knew they had to do something and they had to do it fast. One night when getting Roger ready for bed, Roger had asked them if there was any way possible to move out of their home and never come back. When they asked Roger why he would ask this, his response was something they didn't expect. He had explained that ever since Miss Cunningham died, he hadn't felt safe in Pittsburgh in a very long time. Parents were puzzled on what to do, they knew that Roger had legitimate feelings and they wanted to help him but at the same time they didn't have the money to move. Well that is until November 3, 1989, on that day the family decided to play the Pennsylvania lottery. No one knows why, But something possessed Mr. Burns to purchase a lottery ticket for $56 million. They were watching the nightly news that night when the lottery came on, Mr. Burns' Numbers were: 3, 22, 33, 6 and 17, wouldn't you know it that those are the numbers that popped up on their TV and the best part of it was there with no other winners so they won $56 million clear. The family was more than ecstatic, they finally had enough money to get out of Pittsburgh, The next question was where would they move to with their newfound wealth? They asked Roger what he thought, he thought it over for a second and he said let's go to California. His parents explained that even though they had all of this money now, California was not in the cards because it would be too expensive to live. Roger cried, cried and cried. Finally his parents did give him exactly what he wanted. As soon as the check cleared and all its taxes, the family moved to Sacramento California.

As I had mentioned before, the family had just won the Pennsylvania lottery for $56 million and decided to move to Sacramento California. The family moved to Sacramento August 1, 1989. While there, Anita and Robert start looking for work. Now, I know what you might be thinking, " they just won 56 million, why on earth would they look for work?" let me give you the answer to that question, even though they have the 56 million, they felt that they needed to work just in case things went belly up with the money. Which is pretty smart if you ask this author. Another question you might ask while meeting this book is: why does this guy insist on talking to us during his writing? I have a simple answer for that too, it is simply because I want to engage with my readers and I want them to feel like they can immerse themselves in a story that Itel. Anyway, back to the story. Anita goes on to find work as a nurse at Mount St. Mary's Children's Hospital in the pediatric unit, Robert who had a law degree from the University of Maryland, he went on to work at Cervelli, Cervelli and Robertson law. He was one of the best lawyers in the Pittsburgh area, he doubted himself to be anything like he was at home. He was playing with the big boys now, deep in his heart he knew that it wouldn't be easy competing with some of the guys who have been there for ages. Rodrigo Cervelli and his brother Rigoberto, they have been in the law firm game a combined 24 years and have won over 3 million cases.

Being the busy parents that they were, they were nervous about leaving Roger with the babysitter because of what happened before in Pittsburgh. They knew they had to do something, they just didn't want the same thing to happen again and traumatize their now eight-year-old son. Mr. and Mrs. Burns knew they couldn't forgive themselves if something happened to Roger again, so what they got in the habit of doing was, before they would let anyone babysit Roger, they have them go through an extensive and I mean extensive background check. It was to the point where, you had to figuratively let them stick a cotton swab up your ass and get samples from it in order to babysit Roger. Mr. and Mrs. Burns hated being this uptight about it, but they knew they had to protect their little boy. They thought about sending Roger to another school for traumatized children by the same name of his previous, this was owned by Abigail Cunningham's sister, Morgan Cunningham. The problem was, Roger wouldn't go. Who could blame the little guy though? He couldn't stop thinking about the original Miss Cunningham and how much trust he invested in her, and how he felt that she just up and left him even though it was through no fault of her own. Mr. and Mrs. Burns begged Roger to give it a try, but he refused. However, he did agree to try and go to regular school and make friends. His parents were happy to hear this news, they enrolled him in Theodore Roosevelt school and When it came time to drop him off, the look on his face was that of being scared and excited at the same time.His parents tell him not to worry, that everything will be OK. This is a new town with new people, and there's nothing that he needs to be scared of.

However, his parents as well worried about his well-being. As again, they didn't want to leave him somewhere where he fell uncomfortable. They want to be sure that he will be safe in school, So they hire a private investigator to keep an eye on little Roger. After about a month, Roger tells his parents that he feels he doesn't need to be the protection anymore. He's made plenty of friends and he feels really good at school, Roger finds comfort in playing sports, he takes a real shine to football. His parents I am more than thrilled that he's found his niche, Roger would ask his parents if he could play Baseball and football, they say yes but they also feel a little reluctant. They are reluctant because they know that there are some weird things that go on with sports, they didn't want him touched inappropriately by coaches or anything like that, Roger assures his parents that he will be fine, they also worry because of his seizures but he again tells his parents that everything will be OK, they are worrying for no reason. When trying out for the football team, his coach Marion Douglas, She notices that he has a tremendous amount of speed, she Asks him to try out for wide receiver in which he graciously agrees. At tryouts for wide receivers, he is one of the fastest if not the fastest kid on the team. She asks her daughter who is the starting quarterback, McKenzie Douglas can you throw him a pass deep down field and see if he could catch it, for being so young, she could throw deep bombs with the best of them. She throws the ball about 50 yards down field, and he is able to run underneath and make an incredible one-handed catch. Coach Douglas is more than excited to have him on the team. The team was named the Sacramento Seahawks, the Seahawks hadn't won a championship since 1976. Marion Douglas and her daughter McKenzie joined the Seahawks in 1987, after the original coach John McIntyre was fired due to not letting McKenzie try out for the team because he was a sexist piece of shit.

His first year of football at age 8, he was having second thoughts about playing football because he didn't want to get hurt and he begged his parents to reconsider letting him play. However, Mr. and Mrs. Burns said that if he wanted to play badly then they were going to let him do that. it was really apparent that Roger had gotten himself into a hole, he wanted to make friends but he didn't really want to play football because he was afraid of getting hurt. Roger knew that football was a tough sport, he just didn't know that it was such a rough spot where she found out in practice one day serious he was practicing with his teammates one day and he caught a ball, and he ended up getting blasted by teammate Charlie Kirk. Charlie Kirk was also eight years old, but a big boy for his age. Charlie knew that he had a good chance of hurting Roger, he apologized immediately and said that he didn't mean to hit him that hard. Roger said always forgiven and the two became best friends. At the start of the season, Roger and McKenzie were hot, hot, hot! This School kept track of records at their young age. McKenzie and Roger, They break pretty much every school record that year as far as passing and receiving goes. McKenzie didn't get to start at quarterback until 1989, she spent time on the bench for the 87 and 88 Seasons because of a sexist coach as I mentioned before. The 1989 season, She had 960 yards passing which broke the school record of 700 and Roger had 726 yards receiving which broke the old record tremendously of 433.

Roger was the most targeted receiver on the team, it was evident that Roger and McKenzie had a good rapport. Also with that first season, the duo combined For 26 touchstone which was unheard of at that point. Roger was selected the team MVP by his peers at the end of his first year, his second year however, that would be met with some adversity but he didn't know that yet. Age 9, and his second season he would learn of the passing of his best friend Charlie Kirk, Charlie had childhood leukemia but never let on to anyone that he was sick. Charlie had barely begun life, now it was taken away from him. This upset Roger, something fierce, he refused to eat or he refused to drink anything. Mr. and Mrs. Burns begin to fear that he would shut down again like he did with Abigail Cunningham. They try to cheer him up the best they can, but nothing seems to work. Before losing all hope, They bring in McKenzie, someone that Roger would feel comfortable talking to about how he was feeling. After McKenzie spoke to him, she relayed to his parents that he felt hopeless, He felt that without his best friend life wasn't worth living and he was thinking about quitting football. McKenzie would talk him out of that though, he agrees to come back the next year. Roger and McKenzie worked very hard that season to perfect the good rapport they already have, they decide to make this season about Charlie. Roger agreed to dedicate this season to his best friend, and they won a championship his second season. At age 10, he again thinks about stopping football. McKenzie again is being the voice of reason, she tells him that the team can't get by without him and he agrees to at least play one more season. They will win one more championship in 1991.

November 1991, the family will again move from Sacramento to Atlanta Georgia because Cervelli, Cervelli and Robinson went belly up. No other law firm in the Sacramento area would hire Mr. Burns. Roger however, he doesn't wanna move from his friends. He finally feels comfortable where he is, and after some consideration, they decide to leave him with the Douglas family. This was hard for Mr. and Mrs. Burns but they felt that it would be better not to move him as he's been through the ringer in his young life. Mr. and Mrs. Burns would tell Roger that they would be back to see him very soon, as soon as they could. Unfortunately, when they left on a cold November 23, 1991, Roger would have never thought that would be the last time he would see his parents. Mr. and Mrs. Burns had planned to see Roger a couple months later, they would call Roger and tell him that they would see him soon and Roger couldn't be more ecstatic. The 10-year-old Roger, he waited up all day and all night on that spring day of April 22, 1992, they never made it to him. Roger grew quite sad at this news but it was later found out, on the way to see Roger, the Burns' were in a car accident and his parents didn't survive. Roger again began to shut down, this time the effects from this loss Would greatly affect Roger. Roger began acting out in school, When Marion asked him why, His response was that he didn't feel like being good anymore because his mommy and daddy weren't there. That season of football was his best season, with more than 34 touchdowns in just six games. Three years later at the age of 13, his productivity would increase as the games increased and he did it all without McKenzie, she became a cheerleader because they wouldn't let her play football anymore. However, rather than complain, she just decided to give up the fight . Roger decided that every year after his parent's passing, he would dedicate the seasons to them because he knew it would make them proud.

The next four years were great for him, and at the age of 17 he had tons of college prospects foaming at the mouth to get him. The University of Pittsburgh wanted him, the University of Clemson wanted him, Penn State was taking a look at him, And many many other schools. Despite his slacking off earlier in his life academically at school, His grades now were the best in the school and every school and their grandma wanted Roger to play for their team. Roger, since his grades were so good, he had the option to pull out of school a little bit early and that's what he did but before he would go and choose a college, he would play one more season of football in Sacramento. He has the best season of his lengthy football career, 46 touchdowns and 7092 yards, along with 26 interceptions and 13 defensive touchdowns, and 66 tackles with 36 assists. When it came time to choose a college, he chose a college that wasn't even looking at him full-time but had some interest. That college was the University of Maryland call mom a lot of people wondered why he would choose the University of Maryland and he had explained that it was because his father went there Which a lot of people could understand.

After signing on to be in Maryland Terrapin, Roger figures that because he's a big football star, he could just party all he wants and teachers would do nothing about it. What Roger failed to realize, he was the rookie of the team so he had no upper hand in the situations like he thought he did. Roger started feeling Cressive and he was threatened with permanent expulsion if he didn't clean up his act. Roger would clean up his act and start doing better in classes, he took a degree in children's pediatrics because he wanted to be able to help children in any way that he possibly could. While excelling in his classes, he also excelled on the football field. He told Coach Marty Johnson that he would play any position that Johnson Asked of him, Johnson thought about this and asked him to try at quarterback. One day at practice, He ran into a familiar face, it would be McKenzie Douglas. McKenzie was at the University of Maryland also on a scholarship for volleyball, she was taking classes in order to become a schoolteacher for early childhood education. She also did a lot of cheerleading on the side, when their eyes met again, they ran to each other and gave each other one of the biggest hugs anyone could possibly give. They catch up on old times, and they also admit that they have liked each other for a very long time and they wanted to start dating. After dating for a while, the couple begins to fight about studies and how much Roger parties with his friends and isn't worried about his studies. He tells McKenzie not to worry about him and focus on her fucking studies to quote his words, McKenzie becomes upset and walks out of the room. Later that evening, the couple with reconvene To talk about what happened earlier that day and see if they could make it work. In the midst of conversation, they look deep into each other's eyes. Roger goes in for a kiss, McKenzie will follow and the rest is history if you know what I mean. They make mad passionate love, not once, not twice, not even three times that night, they make love for times in the same night.

Now I know what you're thinking, " four times in the same night, what on god's green earth do you need to do that four times in the night for?" Well, when you're in love, you will definitely do anything to keep the love alive. After their bountiful night of sex, they cuddled for the rest of the night and talked about their future. McKenzie wants to marry Roger, Roger just wants to settle down and focus on football and studying. McKenzie actually gets mad at Roger, she feel that while studying is commendable, she feels that Raju should at least be willing to make a commitment to her. Rodrick gets angry with McKenzie and stormed out of the room, Which leads to another three hours of talking about the future and another two times Roger would get to tap that pussy. A total of six times in one night we had mad passionate sex and Roger decided that McKenzie was right, he didn't need to make a commitment to her and he needed to do it soon. The next day at practice, Coach Johnson was preparing the team for their first game against the University of Pittsburgh Panthers. Coach Johnson didn't know where he wanted Roger to start, every position that he put Roger in, Roger excelled. Coach Johnson finally decides to put Roger and starting quarterback, dethroning the predecessor, Michael Black. Mr. Black had been the starting quarterback for Maryland the last two years, he was more than livid that some rookie could come in and just pick a spot. However, he also understands that the game is played that way sometimes. He agrees to help Roger improve on his throwing and throwing on the run, the question is will he actually help

Roger or will you try to sabotage Roger to get his job back? Surprisingly, Mr. Black will actually help Roger, Roger is extremely grateful for the assistance and advice brought on by Mr. Black. At age 18, he became the youngest starting quarterback in Terrapin history. His debut against The University of Pittsburgh went more than according to plan, 546 passing yards, eight passing touchdowns and one rushing touchdown. The university of Maryland beat the University of Pittsburgh to a pulp with a final score of 63 to 22. Roger's success would not end there, His rookie season was astonishing to say the least. His rookie season finished up with the following stats, 5892 passing yards, 74 passing touchdowns, 22 interceptions and 10 rushing touchdowns. You would think that things for Roger could go nowhere but up from here, but that he hotel keyword of it all, you would think. Things started out good for Roger, but they only got worse. How much worse could they get? Well, I wouldn't be a very good author if I gave all my secrets away right now, now would I? See you in the next chapter!

Well hello there, I see that you made it to the next chapter with me. Congratulations, and most importantly welcome aboard. Now we're weather? Oh yes, things were going quite well for Roger his rookie year. His junior year with more of the same, this dad said fuck off a little bit but still not bad. 4500 yards passing, 56 touchdowns and 25 interceptions, five rushing touchdowns. His studies would fall off greatly though, he went from a straight-A student to getting B's and C's in school. Teachers wonder why this is happening in the attribute it to lack of time to study because of football. Teachers suggest to Roger that he take a break from football for a while, Roger however refuses. Coach Johnson wants him, if he doesn't improve his grades he will be suspended from the team. Roger is furious at the idea that he could be booted from the team, he decides to stop dating McKenzie for a little bit, until he can get his life together. McKenzie is quite furious at the idea, and decides to go out on her own with teammate Michael Black. Michael is thrilled at the prospect of dating McKenzie, Roger however is pissed, and who could blame the young man? Please cause a big rift between Mr. Black, McKenzie and Roger. Roger was furious that McKenzie could move on so quickly, and McKenzie was furious at Roger because she felt that he was neglecting her so she went to someone else who would give her the attention that she thought she deserved.

The affair between McKenzie Douglas and Michael Black didn't last long, Michael became abusive to McKenzie on multiple occasions. Beating and raping the young woman on multiple occasions, when she tried to leave, she would get beaten again. He would be arrested on multiple occasions for McKenzie's abuse but she refused to press charges because she claimed that she loved the man. Roger knew this wasn't true, Roger knew that McKenzie only had eyes for him. One day, Roger took the law into his own hands, he went to Michael Black's apartment and shot him twice in the chest. Roger was arrested later that day, he claimed to have done it for the woman he loved but the police didn't wanna hear it, Since Michael Black died shortly after, Roger was charged with manslaughter. Because of this, Roger had served a year in prison and was booted off the University of Maryland football team for that year. Now you might be wondering, " A year for manslaughter, seems a little late don't you think?" Well let me explain that, it was determined by Judge Henry Peterson to be an active self-defense because he was protecting Miss McKenzie Douglas from a horrible monster in Michael Black. While in prison, Roger continued to work on his football mechanics, passing the ball around with other inmates. He does come particularly close to one inmate by the name of Marty Smith, Marty was imprisoned for the murder of his wife which she did not commit. However, he remained in jail until the start of his new trial. A year later in November, both men were free. Obviously, Roger had lost his starting quarterback job at the University of Maryland, he had to prove to Coach Johnson that he deserved his job back. Because of his relationship with McKenzie or lack thereof, he began drinking heavily. Along with the drinking, there came a use of prescription drugs such as; oxycodone, Percocets, Morphine countless countless others. This was detrimental to his football career and detrimental to whatever shred of a chance he had of getting back together with McKenzie. His football coach had called him that if he didn't string out, there would be no place for him on the Maryland football team. Roger knew this was serious, he had dreams of going to the NFL and he realized hi that if he didn't straighten up and ship out, those dreams would never come true. He agreed with the help of McKenzie and coach Johnson, he agreed to go into rehab for his problem. While in rehab, he continued to work on his studies.

He comes back from rehab, he is stronger and more focused than ever. During that football season, his stats dramatically improved from his Junior year; 64 passing touchdowns, 7800 yards passing, 10 interceptions and 16 rushing touchdowns. Besides his freshman year, this is the best Roger has looked in quite a long time. He even got the love of his life back in McKenzie. The two rekindle The relationship they once had and they couldn't be happier. McKenzie couldn't be happier to have the man she once loved, Cherished and adored. Roger realizes he made a lot of mistakes in their relationship past years and he vows never to make them again. The two of them decide that no matter what happens with the NFL or after college, they are going to be together for a very long time. Roger will play his sophomore year, and again put up astonishing numbers; 8892 yard, 71 passing touchdowns, only six interceptions and 22 rushing touchdowns. This season out of all of them hand NFL scouts foaming at the mouth. He worked out at quarterback for the Pittsburgh Steelers, New York Jets, San Francisco 49ers, New York Giants, New England Patriots and Jacksonville jaguars. He was talking to Bill Callahan, the Steelers head coach at the time, and he was very impressed with Roger's ability to throw on the move and how he has the ability to make very good decisions under pressure. It is the year 2002, he could declare for the NFL draft or stay in school for another year, Coach Johnson wants him to stay another year, McKenzie also thinks that is a good idea. However, Roger really wanted to go to the NFL, he wanted to make your dream come true. It is April 2002, Roger travels to New York City with McKenzie after the scouting combine, Draft night comes and the Jaguars have the first pick, Roger feels like this will be a lock. However, They take defensive back Reginald Johnson out of Clemson. The New England Patriots have the second pick, again he is not chosen, he is not chosen with the first 10 picks. It isn't until the third round that he is selected by the Minnesota Vikings, he begins to wonder why he slid so low in the draft. Roger was told by an NFL scout that's the reason he slid so low, that was because people knew about his past with the drugs and they weren't sure that he would be mentally prepared for the NFL without some type of baggage. He begins to get upset, but then he realizes that it is just an honor to be selected in the NFL and he decides to not complain and keep his mouth shut. After signing a rookie contract and deciding on an agent, Roger goes to Minneapolis Minnesota to the Hubert H Humphrey Metrodome to meet his new teammates. One of the first teammates he will meet would be future Hall of Fame wide receiver Randy Douglas, Randy Douglas should be back in a minute was a tremendous mentor to Roger, Roger was able to perfect his passing, He was able to dethrone starting quarterback again and his rookie year just like in college. Dante Jones lost the starting job to Roger, Head coach Mike Davis was really impressed by Rogers abilities compared to Jones. Dante was saddened to lose his job, but he understood that the NFL is any man's game at any given time. So rather than complain about it, He tries to be the best mentor he can for Roger. Roger quickly discovered the NFL is not like college, his first start gives him a win against the Dallas Cowboys 26 to 23, but that was with four interceptions just a measly 99 yards passing and one touchdown. Roger begins to doubt himself, but McKenzie and Randy Douglas that things will get better. However, Roger Roger things wouldn't get better in his personal life or NFL life. Yes, Roger was headed down a dark road and he didn't even know what yet. One night after practice, The team invited Roger out for some drinks to celebrate the victory against the Miami Dolphins that week. He tried to tell his teammates he didn't drink anymore because of his rough past with booze but teammates kind of made fun of him so he decided to give into peer pressure and go out drinking with the boys at Bobby's bar. McKenzie would beg him not to go, that he knows the consequences of his actions and she doesn't want to see him ruin his chances of the NFL. Roger assured her that he will be fine, he comes home that night drunk as a skunk and begins to sexually assault McKenzie. McKenzie is very upset, she threatens to leave Roger if he doesn't change his ways. The question is, does he love McKenzie enough to change?

Roger would continue to abuse alcohol and painkillers and yet McKenzie continued to try and be patient with Roger, for you see, she was pregnant with their child. Roger was over the moon with joy at the news of her pregnancy. He swears that he will get off of the hooch for good, he does great with that for a while but then he relapses, McKenzie continues to give him multiple chances. After two years of mediocre performance and booze abuse, the Vikings released Roger at the age of 24, Roger is already looking for work in the NFL. He did find work as a backup quarterback to Kelly Testaverde, a 10 year vet of the Pittsburgh Steelers, Rogers gets some sage advice from Testaverde, Testaverde also tells Roger to shape up or he will be out of the league faster than his head could ever spin. Week term 2002, Steelers versus the Cincinnati Bengals. Testaverde starts the game, he ultimately goes down with a knee injury at first glance but is later found out to be a complete ACL tear. Roger is forced to substitute for Testaverde, his first pass was intercepted by defensive lineman Cory Benson and returned for a touchdown. After the initial interception, Roger began to gain confidence and he finished the game with 226 yards passing, four touchdowns and that one interception he threw early. Roger over the next seven weeks compiled; 892 yards, 20 touchdowns and six interceptions, with two rushing touchdowns. The Steelers just missed the playoff window though with a nine and seven record. Even after Testaverde healed, Coach Callahan named Roger the starter for the next season. Testaverde felt this was a good idea as he is getting older and they need a young gun quarterback. His first year as a starter for the Pittsburgh Steelers, he did more than exceed expectations; 4802 passing yards, 38 touchdowns, 10 interceptions and 14 rushing touchdowns. He was returning back to his old form, the question was would he stay that way?

If you answered no to the question I previously asked, you would be correct after his fantastic year as a full-time starter, Roger would hit the hooch yet again. This time McKenzie has had enough, Even though she was nearing the end of her pregnancy with the first child. She leaves Roger until he can clean up his act. The Steelers note his lack and productivity and release the 24-year-old quarterback. Once again, Roger is left looking for work. Many teams bring him in for a work out, many teams turn him away though. Eventually, he gets signed by the Buffalo Bills and head coach Marvin Thomas, Thomas is more than happy to sign Roger so long as he stays off the booze. Roger checked himself into rehab for his problem with alcohol and painkillers, he works really hard to improve himself. McKenzie is impressed, by this time she's had their daughter Emily and agreed to take Roger back. Which time she gave him an ultimatum, get off the booze in pain killers and they could be a family or stay on them and he will never see his daughter Emily again. He swears that he has sipped his last drink, However, he would relapse yet again. Next time, it was so severe that all of his endorsement deals got yanked out from under him. The Buffalo Bills would give him a couple games to straighten out his act but that didn't work and they released Roger Burns, he was blackballed by the NFL and he never took another NFL snap again. He ended up losing the love of his life in McKenzie Douglas, he ended up losing his house and living on the streets, he ended up losing everything because he couldn't put down the bottle. He was only 24 and his life was spiraling out of control. He began to wonder to himself what went wrong and why he was this way. He would attribute it to losing his parents at a young age and just not having the proper support around. He tried explaining this to McKenzie, naturally she didn't want to hear anymore of his excuses and she took visiting rights away from him. So again I ask, how does a 24-year-old football star go from number To a person who is down on his luck? Well when you choose the bottle instead of what's important to you, this may happen. Jager bombs or love, beer or cuddles, Rum or romance. Well if you are Roger Burns you made the wrong decision, You gave up everything for something that will last you five seconds. Alcohol is not worth risking your love.

Chapter 6: life after alcohol

As I said before, Roger had made some questionable decisions, Roger thought drinking was more important than family or football. He was homeless And looking for direction. One day well begging for money on the street, he runs into a young pastor by the name of William Clark, William was the first year pastor at the first church of God in Buffalo New York. He takes Roger under his wing and shows Roger that there is more to life than then Jim Beam, and other alcoholic beverages. He shows Roger that there are people that actually care about him in the world, he attends the church every Sunday and his conditions Start to improve. He's able to find a new job as a taxi driver in Buffalo, he's able to rent a small apartment in the slums of Buffalo. This is not ideally where he wanted to be, but he knows that he brought this on himself. He tries to get a hold of McKenzie, McKenzie doesn't want to hear from him. He begged her to at least let him talk to his daughter but she refused, who could blame the woman? Roger had numerous opportunities to clean up his act, and he refused.

At age 25, things couldn't be looking better for Roger. Roger continues driving taxis,along with making pizzas at Mario's deep dish pizza shop. He was spotted on two different occasions by NFL personnel. One of the people that spotted him, Charlie Hampton, head coach of the Tampa Bay Buccaneers. Hampton had asked Roger if he would consider reviving his career, Roger thought about it for a minute and at the time he said no. His fear was, going back down the same road that got him in the mess he was him prior to making something out of himself now. This would not be the last time he would hear from Hamilton, Hamilton would contact him six more times in order for him to revive his career. Each time Roger declined, Hamilton was relentless though, he didn't like taking no for an answer and he was desperate for a quarterback. The seventh time was obviously the charm, Roger finally agreed to at least try out for the team. Roger got on the next plane to Tampa Bay Florida, when he got there, he was met by Hamilton and some potential new teammates. One of them was the familiar friend, wide receiver Randy Douglas Was traded to Tampa Bay to try and entice Roger to come back.

Roger has a successful workout, he agrees to sign a one-year contract with Tampa Bay on the condition that he stays clean from alcohol and out of trouble. In order to do that, he keeps in contact with him Pastor William Clark just to keep himself on the level. He tries to contact McKenzie again, this time she will allow him to see Emily. Emily is only a year old, when she sees Roger for the very first time she automatically says "dada"! This thrills Roger to no end, McKenzie and Roger start talking about where things went wrong. She explains to him that the reason they broke up was simply because he took more time for alcohol than he ever did for his family. Roger apologized and admitted he was wrong and he would do anything for a second chance. McKenzie is understandably skeptical of his newfound understanding, but she agrees to date him again and see where things go. Roger is grateful for that opportunity.

In the spring of 2007, the couple would wed. McKenzie was more than ecstatic that Roger was clean for over a year, she was beginning to see the Roger that she fell in love with. Emily couldn't be happier to have her father in her life, even though she was almost too, she had a very good understanding of what was going on with her daddy. She would cuddle with him every night and say; " daddy no dizzy juice". That was enough to keep him off the devils juice in combination with keeping in contact with his pastor. His first game as a Tampa Bay Buccaneer was against the Pittsburgh Steelers, Testaverde was still quarterback. He comes over to Roger and says it's nice to see him and welcome back to the league. Roger said thank you, he shook his hand and they went back to their respective sidelines. Roger Have not taken a snap in almost 2 years at the NFL level, He was understandably nervous. At the start of the game, he threw four passes and missed them all. Coach Hamilton was beginning to think that he made a mistake bringing Roger back to the League, however, after the first four misfires he got on target. He was able to compile; 322 yards passing, four touchdowns and one interception in the 28 to 14 win over the Steelers.

After the victory against the Steelers, it was like Roger never missed a step. The next week against the Dolphins it was more of the same deal, 350 yards passing, four touchdowns, no interceptions in a 28-0 win over the Dolphins. As the weeks would go bye, the yardage and touchdowns would continue to go up. At the end of the season, he compiled; 38 passing Touchdowns,

9 interceptions and 5893 yards in passing. He did get Tampa Bay to the playoffs, he ultimately Lost in the NFC championship game to the Green Bay Packers by escrow 24 to 21. Tampa Bay fans were heartbroken but they figured they would try again next year and with Roger back there was no way they could lose. Unfortunately for Roger, he would never get that chance. Not because of drinking, but because during August practice the next year, he tore his ACL and meniscus. He had to have surgery immediately but he was out for The entire 2008 season.

In the spring of 2009, Roger was back but he came with a monkey on his back. His doctor prescribed him painkillers, he was once again going down the road of addiction with those. He tried to kick the habit in the pants because he didn't want to lose everything again but all of his attempts failed. Even rehab didn't help the man, this time McKenzie stayed with him through everything. She realized that in order to keep him somewhat safe, she needed to be around. As Emily got older, she was able to help her father Control his addiction. Roger would still participate with the Tampa Bay buccaneers, he would take them to the playoffs again and reach the Super Bowl, they had won the Super Bowl against the Miami Dolphins by a score of 31 to 7. Roger could not have been more on top of the world than he was that day, That day he realized that he can do anything with the help of his friends. He also realizes that not everyone is your friend regardless how many times they claim to be. He would retire in the spring of 2010 from the NFL. Yes he was still young, but he wanted to take the time to spend with his daughter Emily.

A year later in 2011, one night he began to feel unwell and collapsed on the bathroom floor of his Tampa Bay home. Emily finds him on the bathroom floor an hour later and quickly calls 911. Now, I imagine being Emily and your dad is just laying on the bathroom floor and not waking up. There has to be some pretty scary shit. Paramedics arrive shortly after the car was made, they take him to Saint Alfred hospital in Tampa Where he is in critical but stable condition. After a hospital stay, Roger gets the worst news of his life, Roger finds out that he is suffering from cirrhosis of the liver. This is what happens when you choose alcohol over anything for a long period of time, Roger is given six months to live. The Tampa Bay buccaneers hear this news and are greatly saddened, the whole NFL is saddened by this news and they hold a charity event to raise money for the families medical bills and after he passes if he passes. On March 20, 2011 while he was sleeping, Roger Davis passed away at the age of 29. The streets of Tampa Bay were lined to the gills with people coming out to say goodbye to their quarterback. I said she was put in Raymond James Stadium, the statue was of Roger taking a throwing stance. The plaque read; " Roger Davis, a good man with a heart of gold who went down the wrong path but then came back. He was a good father, a good teammate and a good friend. He will be greatly missed"

Exit

Hello yet again, it's your old pal JJ. I really hope you enjoyed my story. I hope that if there are any alcoholics reading the story, it's OK that you are (well not really) but to each their own I suppose. Just remember, if you choose alcohol over anything you're fighting a losing battle. Especially if that fight is over alcohol or your children, or your wife or your friends or anyone or anything. It is definitely not worth it and the sooner you realize that, the sooner you can get help. Yes I know this book is fictional, but I know there's a lot of people like this. People that would rather have booze then family. I have yet to figure out why that is, but again to each their own. Once again I am JJ and thank you for reading